But they don't
want it in a cup.

They want to eat
it on their face.

i don't want to wear pants

because i never seen

that elephant before.

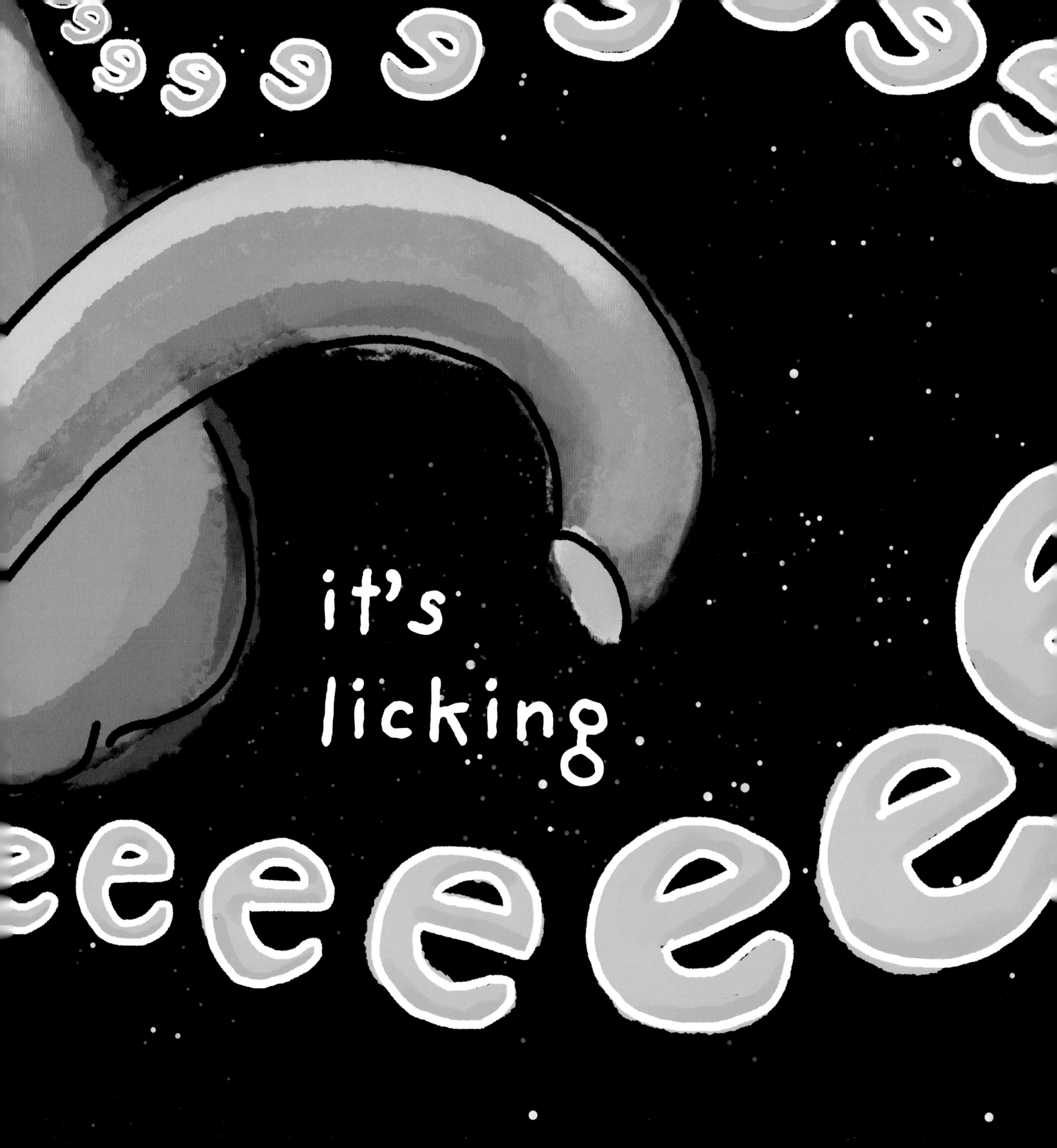

it's
licking

i want to pet them and shoot them to Penny's house.

Can i borrow something from Phoenix?

i am such a big
girl to do this.

Where are the

dead people?

Mo and Z are not here.

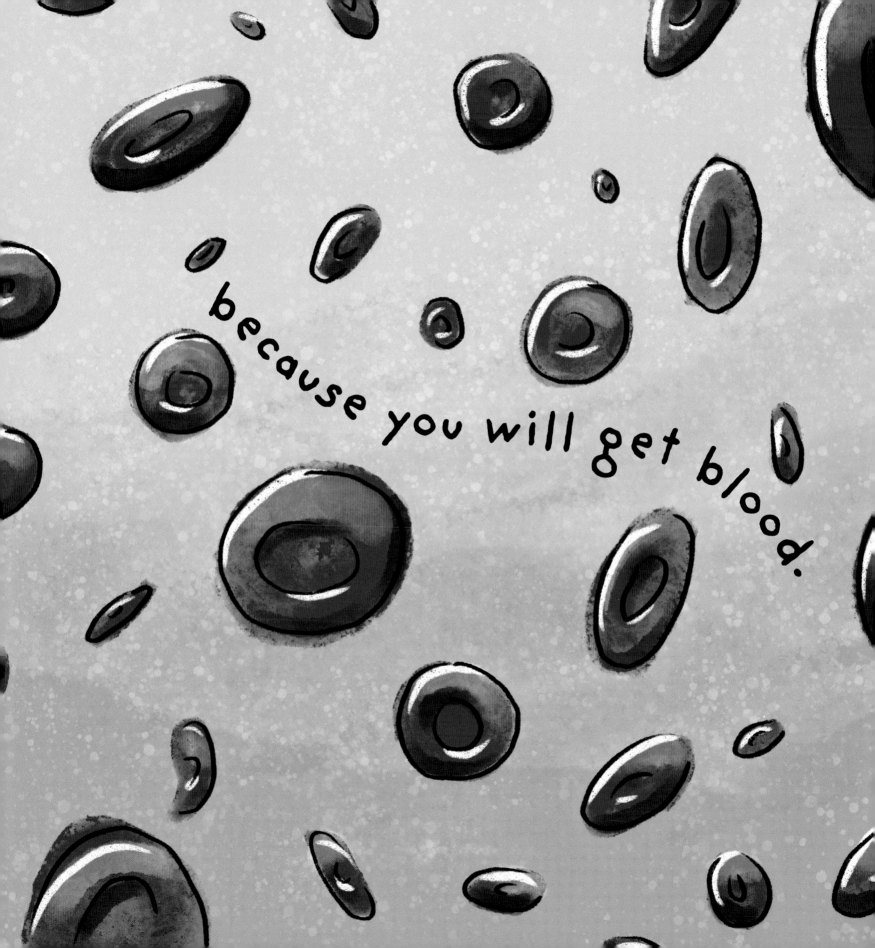

There was a
friendly lion

...and friendly frogs and friendly crocodiles and friendly monsters.

my pets!

but i don't

WANT

to share.

Sharing is caring!

When i
get pushed

my heart
goes away...

and then
i am
SAD.

Let's not talk.

Once upon a
time there
was a papa...

and he had
blue hair.

The
end.

Mélanie Berliet is a writer, producer, and media executive. She is mom to Stella and the General Manager of The Spruce.

melanieberliet.com

Kristina J. Parish makes art, music, and books in Nashville, TN. She is mom to a kid named Mars and likes animals too much to eat them.

kjparish.com

THOUGHT CATALOG Books

Copyright © 2021 Mélanie Berliet. All rights reserved.

Published by Thought Catalog Books, an imprint of the digital magazine Thought Catalog, which is owned and operated by The Thought & Expression Company LLC, an independent media organization based in Brooklyn, New York and Los Angeles, California.

This book was produced by Chris Lavergne and Noelle Beams. Art direction, illustration and design by KJ Parish. Visit us at *thoughtcatalog.com* and *shopcatalog.com*.

978-1-949759-37-2

Made in the United States of America.